A message from t

To all of my black queen   **t
anyone tell you any differ**   **....autiful. Black
is strong. Black is natural. No matter what shade of
black you are, you are beautiful a gift from God and
don't forget that.**

This song and story are for you

Hold up your crowns queen's xx

Peng Black Girls remix – Enny ft. Jorja Smith

There's Peng black girls in my area code
Dark skin, light skin, medium tone
Permed tings, braids, got mini afros
Thick lips, got hips some of us don't
Big nose contour, some of us won't
Never wanna put us in the media, bro
Want a fat booty like Kardashians? (No)
Want a fat booty like my aunty got, yo (Ayy)
Wheel up the bloodclart, tell her reload it
I've got the camera, my girls are posin'
I need some back up then my ones are rollin'
Grown woman ting, so I'm never at risk
Mind my own business so I'm never in mess (Uh)
Who am I? I ain't bait (Oh)
Get a slice of the cake
Want a house with a view and a new pair of shoes
Keep it real from the jump
Gucci gang, Lil Pump

Little vibe, little bass, little kick, little snare
Little lies, big truths
Do you, they don't care
Do you, they don't care
Get your ass out the box and build up from there
I don't have a gang with me
But I still walk with a gangster lean
And rock Nike's cause we think they're clean
MJ, leather jacket, beat it, Billie Jean
MJ, leather jacket 'cause I think I'm bad
That's cool, I like it
The growth, the light
The pain, the fight
We love, we fight
We hurt, we cry (*No, no*)
He paid the price
You'll be alright

I think I need some time away
I took a little time, I prayed
We gon' be alright, okay
Alright, okay
Alright, okay
I think I need some time away
I took a little time, I prayed
We gon' be alright, okay
Alright, okay
Alright, okay
Alright, okay

ENNY said there's peng black girls in our area codes
These black girls need to be in the shows

Be on the runways, not just mood boards
On top of that, we gotta see them in your team
Look at your crown, natural relaxed
Had a Jheri curl one time, soft and sheen
Where black girl magic is sometimes blue
Might have broke a hair band or two
Raise my voice, you gonna say that I'm angry
Kiss my teeth and now you say that I'm hood
Kid at sixteen, you say it's my destiny
Drive a Range, you think I'm up to no good
Give us a break and let us breathe, man
Give us a chance, let us achieve, fam
And I know that my hair looks a bit different today
So don't touch my hair
Like, new hair, who this?
Old black bomber jacket and the Bantu twists
Look, mind over matter, I can handle this
We're fine, took a second, the rewards in risk
See, I think that I care too much
Bottle of some Covousier, two cups
I've got nothing to show but you love to check my flaws
and all my trials
I was black back when it wasn't even in

That's cool, I like it
The growth, the light
The pain, the fight
We love, we fight
We hurt, we cry
He paid the price
You'll be alright

I think I need some time away
I took a little time, I prayed
We gon' be alright, okay
Alright, okay
Alright, okay
I think I need some time away
I took a little time, I prayed
We gon' be alright, okay
Alright, okay
Alright, okay
Alright, okay

Acknowledgments

I would like to thank these people for helping me push and continue to write. After being discouraged and had stopped writing, these two people got on my ass and pushed me.

Jaz

Jaz thank you sooo much for pushing me, even though you live in America and our time differences would mess us up. You continued to push me everyday, you prayed for me when I was feeling down. You made me believe that the world needed to hear my stories. You are my sister for life, continue to push Jaz don't let anyone or anything stop you from living your dream, because if u do I'm personally coming to America to kick your ass. Thank you for everything. There is more I need to say but I can't put them on here. You never know he may be watching lol.

Anasha

Anasha thank you for putting up with my moaning and my constant disbelief in myself while writing this book and in general. Our late night conversations when I would get mad at you because you were trying to help me but I was being too stubborn to listen. Thank you for not giving up on me. You know you my sister, I've been saying this for years now. Thank you baby girl. You are an inspiration to me Nash, I see where your going and I love it.

Chapter 1

rystal

March 6th 2014

"Krystal, get your black ass out of this bed right now, you're going to be late for school !!" My grandmother shouted at the top of her lungs.

Today is an exciting day for me because today I start a new school. In my old school it was mainly white kids and they teased me about the colour of my skin. They never teased my sister or any of the other black girls at my school. It was just me because I was darker than the rest of them and when I say darker, I mean I was a deep deep rich chocolate colour. I was the darkest in my family, darker than my mother (may she rest in peace), grandmother and especially darker than my younger sister Katrina who was a beautiful rich caramel colour. Her skin would glisten in the sunlight, oh how I wish I had her skin colour and not my own. I was burnt and ugly, 'I was too dark for a black girl' as my grandmother would always tell me. When my mom was alive, she made me feel like my skin signified royalty, she would always say, "Krystal you are a queen just like the Nubian queens before us, your skin is rich just like theirs. Embrace it".

When she died, I no longer had anyone remind me that my skin was the skin of a Nubian queen, my grandmother would say in a jokingly way, "You were burnt when you were little, your mother left you outside too long" or she would say "you better be smart in school because no man is ever going to take a burnt woman as his wife just look at mine and your sisters skin tone." I would look at my grandmother puzzled when she mentioned a husband because she had three kids with three different men and didn't have a husband, so I don't understand her point at all.

"You better get up Krystal, you know how she is in the morning," said Kat. Kat, is my sister and best friend all rolled into one even though we are 18months apart. I was born in March 1993 and she was born in September 1994, so in school terms she is two years below me.

"Kat I'm up already, I'm just trying to mentally prepare myself for today. You know new school and all and on top of that what if these guys are just like the kids in my other school? Sis I'm scared."

"What you got to be scared about? I'm going to be right there with you, we're walking into this new school together, the only time I'm leaving you is when we're in class because obviously we're not in the same year Rissy. I will never leave you, if anyone tries to bully you about the tone of your skin, just remember what mum used to say to you."

"You are a queen just like the queens before us, your skin is rich just like their skin, embrace it, yes yes I hear you."

"Krystal, I know your burnt black ass is not still not dressed for school, look at your sister she's dressed and ready to go." My grandmother said whilst barging into my room.

You see, this is how I constantly get reminded that my skin is not worthy – verbal abuse from my grandma.

"Grandma, she's not burnt please stop saying that, she is beautiful." Katrina butted in.

"She may be beautiful but she is darker than me and you, compared to us her skin looks burnt. What? Do you want me to lie?"

"No grandma," Katrina said, shaking her head.

"Right, what do I always tell you to do? To tell the truth and what...?"

"Shame the devil" we both said in unison, I guess there was a compliment somewhere in what she said, I think.

Walking through the big iron gates we entered George Dixon International School and Sixth form Centre or as everyone else calls is G.D. The first thing I noticed when I walked onto the school field was the array of different nationalities, but the best part about it was that I was not the only dark-skinned black girl there.

Over the years I attended G.D I felt happy at that school even though Kat and I were never close whilst in school, we still remained best friends outside of it. It was all due to the fact that we both had different sets of friends that we hung with. She hung out with the popular girls and I, well let's just say I'm a part of the 'three musketeers' as everyone called us. There was John; he was known as the teddy bear or the blob. Can you guess how he got that name? You guessed right it's because he was the largest person in the school. Then there was Monica; she was known as Einstein because she was super smart. Then there was me, can you guess what my name was? Yup, you guessed it right they called me midnight. Even the teachers called me midnight, I think they thought it was my nickname or something, I would complain to my grandmother about this but all she would say is "girl you are black like midnight, if you really want to do something about it then I will buy you some bleaching soap or bleaching cream so you will shut up about it."

Yes, you are reading correctly, she did say she will buy me some bleaching products.

Can you imagine that type of energy she was giving off and all the degrading and belittling she and everybody else had done to me, it went on for another 2 years at school and another 4 years in college, I could handle myself at college than in school, since I just sat there in my little corner nobody really bothered me apart from the silly little boys who found it funny to pick on everyone. But you see I have a plan; I know that in 5/10 years they all will be working for me and I can't wait.

atrina

My grandmother was always the hardest on my sister, I never understood why she would make her feel like her skin colour was anything but beautiful. I wish she could see the beauty that I can see, my sister has the most memorising dark skin I have ever seen in my life, it looked so pure and untouched as if God himself had painted her.

I wish I had her skin colour. It was so magical, when the sun hit her skin, she would glow and it only enhanced her beauty.

My skin now was dull and pale, nothing magical about it at all. I was more on the light side of being black. My skin shade was borderline white, I looked see-through.

Looking at my sister, I was fully aware that she would get bullied about her blackness, which I thought was crazy. She always thought that I had it easy, but little did she know she was not the only one who was teased about their skin... I was as well. People always told me that I was 'too white' and 'I don't have an ounce of black in me' or 'I'm a white girl trying to be black'.

It was crazy to me because I knew I was black. Both of my parents were black but deep down I never felt like I was black enough. I always thought that God forgot to dip me longer in that melanin pool.

When college started boys started to notice me more. They loved my light skin. The only thing that still was hard was me maintaining my confidence. See what people never knew about me was whenever I went on holiday I absolutely loved when my skin tanned. I turned it into a nice light chocolate colour. Do I wish I could tan darker heck yeah! I know you meant to love yourself but being light, I could not.

I blame my grandmother for that. If only she loved and embraced all shades of black, then maybe just maybe I could appreciate my colour more.

Chapter 2

<u>Present day 1st October 2021</u>

atrina

Black history month October 1st. Every year we celebrate our black history, and I hated it. I never hated it for the reasons you would think, no, not because of slavery, well, yes, it is because of that. Every year I was reminded of the fact that my great great great great great grandmother was raped by a slave master and that's why my skin was so light. I never knew the reason why it was so light until I went to secondary school and that shit was put on full blast. My skin colour was a product of rape and I hated it. The whole world is messed up, they praise us light skins and say our skin is beautiful but never want to acknowledge the fact that are tone of skin was passed down to us because a white man decided he wanted to rape the pretty black girl because his white wife was not fucking him right or enough at home.

I know it may seem like I hate white people but I don't because one of my best friends is white and she's blacker than me. Let me explain what I mean by that, yes, her skin colour is white but she was raised by a black family ever since she was 1 years old, they adopted her, Brianna is 100% white on the outside but on the inside she 1100% black, and 9 times out of 10 you get the black version of her the only time you get the white version is when she has to use her telephone voice, you guys know the voice I'm talking about.

Walking into my job at Ikea I loved my job role there, I was the interior designer. I wanted to be an interior designer. It was my dream job. Walking around the shop floor I bumped into my assistant Olivia. She was pretty, she was the same skin tone as me. She had a nice grade of hair but she always wears wigs, her wigs were always extra like today she had a blonde wig on. The only thing different was the tips of her hair. One side was red and the other was blue, she reminded me of Harley Quinn with that hair style.

"Hey Liv, did you manage to sort out the bedroom display?"

"Yes, I did, and I also did the living room display as well"

"Thank yo..."

"Excuse me, do you have these sheets in queen size please?"

I swear to God, this is the most handsome customer I have ever seen. He was a beautiful dark brown colour, pretty white teeth, he looked to be about 6ft2, he also looked like he had a strong back if you know what I mean and that deep sexy Barry White voice. He reminded me of Morris Chestnut in The best man. Oh, my lawd.

Before I could even open my mouth and answer this fine specimen Liv opened her mouth and answered.

"Yes, we do they are over here let me take you to them"

"Thank you," replied the unknown customer. Both of them walked off towards the area the sheets were.

I love days like this when the shop is not busy, I can really focus on my display designs. I could not wait to leave this job though and I started working for myself, I have big dreams. Working here is just a means to an end really, I feel it in my bones that I'm going to blow up and nobody will be able to reach me.

As I stood at the counter, I realised that Liv was gone awhile now, normally I would not have noticed but she did walk off with that sexy motherfucker earlier. As I was wondering where she had gotten to, I heard a little giggle, that giggle I knew all too well it was Liv's giggle she would do when she was flirting with somebody or was trying to steal somebody's man, as she always did. Don't get me wrong I'm not trying to judge anyone but the way how I see it is that, you're a beautiful girl, why don't you find your own man and not steal anyone else's man. I really don't understand women like that, but I, not in denial I know that it's all so the man's fault as well because he should have been more faithful in the first place, but still ladies if the man is taken all ready and you like him leave it alone go an find your own man. You home wrecking bitches blow me.

"Make sure u come to the party and bring some friends with you"

"Oh, I will, and you make sure you ring me later on"

"You don't have to worry about that," he said while chuckling.

 I swear it was the sexiest chuckle I have ever heard before in my life. Yes, I can hear it guys. I know I sound crazy right now.

"You can come if you like," he said while handing me a leaflet promoting his party. "Me?"

I asked with a puzzling look on my face. I know he could not be talking to me, not this fine ass specimen.

"Yes you, bring a couple of your friends as well"

"She doesn't have any pretty friends," Liv said while rolling her eyes.

"She only hangs with her burnt looking sister" she grumbled.

She must have thought she whispered that part because her face turned a shade of red when Nubian king cleared his throat. She must have thought that the comment was funny because she was the only one laughing.

I was seeing RED!! This bitch has taken one too many shots at my sister's skin tone. How can a bitch be all about embracing yourself and have a #blackgirlmagic t-shirt, bracelet, mug basically every black girl magic thing you can think of and here she is tearing down a black ~~woman~~ queen? Can someone say fraud. As Marlo Hampton from Real wives of Atlanta said to Eva Marcille in Tokyo 'you're a fraud '.

I walked right up to her face and spoke

"Bitch say one more thing about my sister, I dareeeee you to say something. Cause I can say fuck this job and have another job lined up in a second unlike you. Bitch we can go if you want".

When I tell you, I was ready to say fuck this job just so I can fuck her up, I meant every single word. I don't play about my sister.

This bitch rolled her eyes and walked away scary hoe. I was about to walk away when I heard somebody cough. I looked to the right of me and this man was still standing there OMG! I wanted to run away, but you did what I did instead.

"I am sorry sir, that was really unprofessional of me. For your inconvenience I'll give you a 10% discount on the stuff that you have purchased today"

"Nah you good, don't worry yourself about it just make sure that you and your friends come to my party"

He gave me the flyer for his party and he walked off. I stood there standing with my mouth wide open. This sexy man just walked off leaving me lost for words. I could feel the seat of my panties getting wet, what the fuck is this man doing to me?

Later at the party

Arriving at the venue I pulled up in my 2019 q3 Audi I looked at myself and my sister and I must say we were looking very cute in our outfits. She wore a black floral flared sleeve tie waist playsuit with gold T-bar pointed toe sandals and gold accessories and I wore a yellow off the shoulder playsuit with black T-bar pointed toe sandals and black accessories.

"Pon di bed u afi try me, try fi catch dis

Bedroom bully yea

Pon di bed u afi try me, try fi catch dis

Bedroom bully

And mi pum pum tun up

You fi get back shot, fat ass smack dat

Waistline grip dat, bip bop tek dat

Turn around and lip lock, gyal u make di dick drop

Body in a tip top, wrestle with di big shot

That's a bad bitch dat if she mad I fix that

She deserve to good shag, she deserve so whole bag

She deserve di whole day, she deserve di 4 play

Make love on a bed of money shawty you afi try me

Pon di bed u afi try me, try fi catch dis

Bedroom bully yea

Pon di bed u afi try me, try fi catch dis

Bedroom bully

And mi pum pum tun up"

"Bitch this my song" I said to Krystal as we entered the party.

I swear this was some boujee ass party everything from the decorations to the food being catered, they had white rice, rice and peas, plantains, bammy, oxtail stew, mutton, KFC, prawns, mac and cheese, crab's, lobster, salmon, brown stew chicken, steam fish and crackers escovitch fish oxtail steam cabbage, jerk chicken, saltfish, callaloo and curry chicken. Don't get me started, on the stage there was a throne in the middle of the stage and a big banner above it which said 'Happy Birthday King Troy' with a crown above the 'y' in this name.

We went to go and get some drinks from the bar because the way we were dancing to Teejay and Ishawna's song mood, we needed these drinks. The DJ was playing the hell out of these tunes. I swear he was only playing these types of songs so the man dem and whine up behind us females, well what do you expect when you turn up at a yardie party.

"All the gyal dem who have dead buddy at home and him nuh no what fi do, ah dis yah fi say to him" the DJ shouted over the music.

"What they say sis?" I asked Krystal

"Mi neck ready fi a choke hold

Grab mi an' fuck out mi pure soul

Mi cum fi hood fyah

But yuh fuck mi all night

Lik seh yuh a burn coal

Yeee

Push yuh cock inna mi nose hole

Rub out mi back pon di cold floor

Yeee

Mi cum fi hood fyah

But yuh fuck mi all night

Lik seh yuh a burn coal" Krystal sang

"Bitch did she just say shove cocky ina har nose hole" I said while laughing

"Why would I want a dick in my nose? My nose is too small for a dick to be going up there. I have two holes on my body they can use, leave my nose hole alone" I said while drinking my rum punch. While making my comment about my nose hole being too small for a dick to be in there Krystal spat her drink out and some of it ended on all on my legs and a little bit on my outfit.

"I'm so sorry but that was too funny. Do you want me to follow you to the bathroom?"

"Nah I'm ok just wait for me here I should not be long"

As I made my way to the bathroom, I bumped into something rock hard. I had to hold my nose and blink my eyes a couple of times because my senses had gone all funny. As I looked up, I saw the birthday boy he was wearing the hell out of the three-piece suit he was wearing. This man had the audacity to wear a crown on his head and had a pimp stick in his hand, he had a chain around his neck. He knew he looked fine as hell.

My heart was beating so hard out my chest, just looking at him made my mouth water. I had to touch the corner of my mouth just to make sure there was no saliva coming out.

The energy between us was like electricity. The sparks bouncing off us reminded me of a faulty wire that had been cut. It felt like all the air in the room had been sucked out and I was finding it hard to breathe. Why is this man doing this to me? We had only met yesterday, so I never understood why he was making me feel like this. The seat of my thong was now soaking wet. I definitely needed to change my underwear and have a cold shower.

"You ok there beautiful? You need to watch where you are going." He said while giving me a wink.

"Hey I remember you, you're the little cutie I met yesterday at Ikea? The one who was about to beat the life out of Liv init?"

Shit he had to remember me by that init. Now he's going to look at me as the 'angry black woman'. If defending my sister makes me an angry black woman then so be it.

Now that I think about it, how does he remember Liv's name and not mine? Well, I guess I can't be mad because he was talking to her for a while and they did plan to meet up later on that day, I swear Olivia Mcken would fuck a horse if she could. That girl loves dick so much it would not surprise me if they fucked after she left work.

She was a mess, not that I'm hating on the girl cause I'm not. Plus, there is nothing to hate on. The thing with Liv is she can't seem to keep a man longer than 2 months, but yet has 3 kids for 3 different men to make matters worse she doesn't have custody of any of her kids.

I mean she is a pretty girl and I can see how someone would be interested in her but when they find out about her mouth, it's game over.

"I was not going to beat the life out of her, teach her a lesson maybe. I don't play about my sister"

"I hear that and I respect that you defended your sister. But on another note, who you come with and are you enjoying the party?"

"I came with my sister and yes I'm enjoying myself, maybe enjoying myself a little bit too much, some drink spilled on me."

"Is that why you were heading in this direction? I thought it was because you were finally coming over here to speak to me. I noticed you as soon as you came into the party, you telling me you never noticed me?"

He said with a grin on his face.

"I noticed.... that big ass banner and throne you have up there" I said while giggling.

He was about to say something back to me but he turned around and was met with a kiss on the cheek by none other than Liv. I swear this girl has the worst timing ever.

"Happy birthday Troy, you look really sexy tonight," said Liv

"Thanks Liv"

"Oh, hi Katrina" she said while rolling her eyes "I see you made it. I see your sister brought your sister as well"

Ok where is this bitch going with this and why is she bringing up my sister?

"She looks nice in her little yellow outfit or whatever" she said.

"On that note Troy it was nice seeing you again, enjoy the rest of your birthday" I said, and with that I walked away because I was not about to entertain this bitch any more.

Chapter 3

Krystal

While waiting for my sister to come back from the bathroom, I decided to go back to the food table and get some more food. Halfway there my favourite song came on and I started singing from the top of my lungs as this song speaks out to me in ways no one will understand.

"Breaking news

Man wan' kill him gyal, ah guess ah 'cause her pussy too good

Breaking news

Gyal yuh pussy too good

Breaking news

Man wan' kill him gyal, ah guess ah 'cause her pussy too good

Breaking news

Gyal yuh pussy too good

If yuh's ah king, treat her like ah queen

'Member seh now di two ah unuh ah like ah team

Don't be di man weh just cyan understand

Him nuh born wid ah pussy and ah gwan like ah fi him

Stop fight wid him

Mek him fight for yuh like Tyson, girl (Like Tyson)

Yuh too nice to him

Di bwoy love him belly, poison him" I sang.

If you're wondering why this song speaks to me, I'll give you a little back story on my first and last relationship for now maybe. I was with this guy named Aaron. At first, he was the nicest, sweetest guy you could ever meet, then halfway through our relationship he started to get really aggressive. He would shove me here and there and call me names. One night he punched me in my face which caused my eye to swell and my lip to bust open. He said the reason why he had done it is because I'm a black bitch and he was tired of fucking on some burnt pussy, even though the pussy was good it was still burnt. Every other night this continued he would get mad and fight me and then he would apologise for it and I would forgive him, all in the name of love. I used to make excuses as to why my face was the way it was and I would deny the fact that he was putting his hands on me.

Aaron was a great guy when he never got mad. I used to believe that he was my soul mate and he only used to say and do these things to me when he would get angry just like my grandmother used to.

He would always convince me to stay with him. He would say 'I love you Krystal I just get angry at the things you do and say, but you know my heart is with you always'. He would say that every time after he would fight me.

I used to hide black eyes and bruises on my body from Katrina, and yes the bruises did show up on my dark skin but not as much as it would show up on a person with lighter skin than mine. I guess it's a benefit to having dark skin then, when the blood travels to the surface of my skin it's not that noticeable.

One night I cooked him a surprise dinner because I had something I had to tell him. I made us loaded mash potatoes with all the trimmings and steak with asparagus. The evening was going so well until I told him I had a surprise, I was pregnant. As soon as I told him I was pregnant I felt a fist connect to my face and my left eye instantly swelled up. I was rolling on the floor holding my eye as tears started to come out of my eyes. I was about to speak when his foot came crashing down on my stomach. I will never forget the words he said while he was stomping on my stomach 'I don't want this baby it's going to come out crispy just like you, I lost a bet and get stuck with you and now you're telling me I'm going to be stuck with you forever, fuck that. You better get rid of this baby'.

I could not believe the man I was so deeply in love with was doing this to me again, but not only was he doing it to me he was doing this to our unborn child.

I don't know how but somehow I managed to gather the strength to stand up and run into the kitchen to get the biggest knife I could find. I stabbed him in his arm and his leg, there was so much blood I don't even know if it was his alone. We started tussling and just when I started to feel my strength diminish the front door was kicked open and in walks the police and they arrested him on the spot.

I was brought to the hospital because as you can guess, I was losing the baby, I also had dislocated my hip bone and a broken rib. I later found out that it was his neighbour who called the police. To be honest that particular neighbour had called the police to his house before as he could always hear me screaming for help in there.

That experience alone let me know men only want light skin girls and us dark skin girls are a joke.

Aaron is now in prison for attempted murder. He writes to me and tries to phone me asking for me to come and see him, I can never bring myself to reply to any of his letters. I do however answer his phone calls not all the time, I think I have what Bell in Beauty and Beast has. Stockholm syndrome is a real thing you guys. I finally feel like I have broken out of it.

Getting back to the party I got some more food and made my way back to the bar. Katrina was taking forever to clean herself up after I spat my drink at her. The music was banging and so was the food, I was definitely going to find out who cooked all this food and get their number.

A song I have not heard in a long time came on and everyone went crazy.

"Wicked, wicked, Junglist massive

Wicked, wicked, Junglist massive

Wicked, wicked, Junglist massive

Wicked, wicked, original

Well big up

All the original Junglist massive

The original dancehall junglist dere

General Levy alongside the MBeat

The world is in trouble

Ah what we tell dem murdera

It goes

I am the, incred' incred' Incredible General

Sensational wah dem call me

Incred' incred' Incredible Gene'

Select, selec'lect"

I kid you not as soon as those words came on every female and males hands instantly turned into gun fingers and everyone was doing the sniper pose. If you don't know about the sniper pose then you should not be listening to my story because you are too young. My garage heads know about this song and the sniper pose. If you know about this song and the pose, do the pose one time with me right now.

Did you do it? because I did.

Dancing a bit too hard to incredible I stepped back and accidentally stepped on someone's shoes. I kid you not my anxiety went sky high because stepping on someone's shoes could end up turning into a fight breaking out which could end up with someone getting stabbed and someone losing their life.

I turned to look behind me to see who's shoe I stepped on so I could apologise to them. I looked up and I saw the most handsomest man I have ever seen in my whole entire life. This man was so beautiful looking at him he looked just like Terrence Howard in Hustle & Flow. The tattoo on his neck looked like it was an extension of his skin.

His cologne was invading my nose, it was Tommy Hilfiger Impact Intense. I only knew because that was the same cologne Aaron used to wear. My whole body froze thinking Aaron was around but I had to tell myself that he is still locked up in prison and he can't get out.

"I am so sorry for stepping on your shoes" I said to the handsome man.

"It's ok sweetheart, no harm no foul done. I saw you getting your sniper on so I can understand" he said while chuckling

Omg I feel so mortified I know I'm not the best dancer around but I do try my best to shake a leg.

"Omg please don't, I feel so ashamed right now" I said while covering my face.

"Nah don't feel ashamed it's cool no one noticed you having a seizure"

"Please stop, was it that bad?"

"Nah I'm messing around with you" he said while chuckling. "Damien, nice to meet you" he introduced himself while shaking my hand.

"Krystal"

"Krystal, I like it, that name suits you. A gem just like you" he said while licking his lips.

"Oh, wow you got your finessing game tight I see" I said while smirking.

"Nah not even, I just find you really beautiful for dark skin girl and I'm really intrigued"

Did he really just say I'm beautiful for a dark skin black girl?

"What do you mean for a dark skin girl?" I asked him.

My face was now visibly showing that I was very displeased with what he said. I hate when someone of colour turns around and says 'oh I don't think you should wear that shade of colour it does not suit your skin tone' or 'you don't need to wear any make-up, you would look like a clown'.

I was fed up with it. It really be your own people who degrade you even more than any other race. My sister and my mother were the only two people who loved my skin. I know this may sound like I'm contradicting myself, but it really hurts when a fellow black person tells me I'm too dark or I'm pretty for a dark skin girl. What makes it worse, it's the ones whose mom is as dark as me, but they think dark skin girls are ugly. Erm excuse me your mom is dark skin so what you saying she's ugly? Make it make sense please.

I don't know what it is about the black community, well I cant just say its the black community because I know for a fact that the Asian (Indian) community has the same problem as well. I had this neighbour we had when I was younger her name was Priya. I remember like it was yesterday her older Reena sister was getting married, she looked so beautiful her skin was like milk. She looked so flawless, the henna complimented her skin so well. She was decked out in gold jewellery. She wore the prettiest red Lehenga I have ever seen in my life, and with the road we used to live on I had seen my fair share of them.

Anyway, I remember Priya's aunty telling her she would never marry because she was too dark and nobody wants a dark ugly wife, she told her that if she did marry it would be to someone who came from a poor family as she will not attract an established man. Ain't that some shit.

"I ain't mean nothing by it, imma be honest I don't normally get attracted to dark skin girls but it's something about you I can't put my finger on it"

I was about to respond to what he said until all I heard was.

"This my shit" he said while moving his hips in a number eight figure.

No tiene la culpa

Amor de compra y venta

Amor de en el pasado

Bem, bem bem bem, bem bem bem

Bem, bem bem bem, bem bem bem

Trapping like narco

(narco)

Got dope like Pablo

(Pablo)

Cut throat like Pablo

(cut throat)

Chop trees with the Draco

(Draco)

On the nawf, got Diego

(Diego)

Say hasta luego

(Luego)

Muy bien wrap a kilo

(yhh)

Snub nose with potato

Straight out the jungle

This man was dancing hard to bamboleo x narcos – (nalo remix). I'm not going to lie that was a big tune still, when that beat dropped it just did something to you.

I turned to my left and I saw my sister walking back towards me with a hard face. I knew that face that was the 'imma bout to fuck somebody up' face. So, I grabbed my food. I was so happy that it was in a takeaway box, and I walked out the party with my sister on my heels. I could hear her mumble something in the background but I could not hear her due to the music still being too loud.

We reached my car and I could see the steam coming off her body, so I knew somebody had royally pissed her off.

"Wait wait Katrina, where are you going?"

I looked up to see who was calling my sister's name, and to my surprise it was the birthday boy. Now my antennas were going off, why is he calling my sister and why is that jackass Damien with him.

"Katrina, why are you leaving the party?"

"Troy, I can't stay cause if I do imma catch a case and that wont be good for anyone, so imma step away before shit gets sticky"

"Wait sis who are you trying to fight?" I asked as I was hella confused at what was going on.

"Liv's thot ass. She be making too many comments and I'm tired of it"

I made an 'O' with my lips and nodded my head. Now I understand what was going on. I also understood what she wasn't saying as well. I knew Liv would have to make a comment about my skin tone and she was always passive-aggressive with it as well.

"Imma talk to her about it"

"I don't need you to do that Troy I can fight my own battles I don't need your help"

"O.K. I hear that but still I'll talk to her anyway cause she out of line anyway, plus sis is beautiful so I know Liv is talking bare shit"

With his hand sticking out towards me he tried to introduce himself to me but I just gave him my resting bitch face and he chuckled.

"I see you mean, sis, but you have nothing to worry about"

"Nah bro she's not mean, she just pissed off with a comment I made while talking to her in there, but I don't know why when it was a compliment". Damien said.

"Your pretty for a dark skin girl is not a compliment. What sort of backhanded compliment is that? You know what don't answer that, Rina, I'll be in the car".

That man was bat shit crazy if he thought I was going to take that. The reason why I'm so mad about what he said is because he made me feel so small, oy was the same feeling Aaron used to make me feel, and I hated that feeling.

I sat in the car waiting for Katrina to finish her conversation with Troy. I guess he said the right things to her because I saw her type in her number and vice versa. All while Damien kept staring at me, which made me feel all tingly inside. Hey, I'm human and he is fucking gorgeous, but I'm still not feeling what he said

Chapter 4

𝒦rystal

It was a beautiful warm November day. I know what you're thinking. It's November. How is it warm? well welcome to England. Where the season's are backwards and it snows in March. Katrina and I decided to take a nice drive up to Nottingham just to visit our grandmother. She had moved back to Nottz to be closer to her siblings. I remember the day she left I cried so much that I ended up giving myself an anxiety attack, grandma was mean with her approach. She came out with 'why are you acting like that burnt Barbie? Stop acting a fool now'. I cried because in a weird way I was going to miss her mental abuse. I guess that's properly why and how I ended up with someone like Aaron.

"Say I wanna leave you in the mornin'
But I need you now, yeah, yeah
I find you, I give you all you needin'
I know you what you like
I feel it comin'

Time is of the essence
I tried to teach you
But I might need some lessons
I need to give it all
I tried to leave but I can't
I don't know why, you're the one
Turn me out of my mind"

Katrina sang, she was singing her heart out to Wiz kid's new song Essence. That song definitely had been our summer jam.

It had been 5weeks since the party where I met that obnoxious sexy chocolate of a man and his brother. I never wanted to see him again, but at the same time I did.

At the corner of my eye, I could see Rina smiling like a Cheshire cat. If she never stopped smiling like that then she would have a permanent smile on her face just like the Joker, there has to be a reason why she's so happy and I'm going to get to the bottom of it.

"Who's got you smiling like that Rina?"

"Somebody"

This bitch.

"Does this somebody have a name?"

"Yeah, he does I just don't think I should tell who it is"

"And why not, unless it that bum bitch Liv then you can keep that"

I swear I hated that girl. I know you're not meant to hate anyone but it's something about her that really upsets my spirit. I'm the type of person who goes off energies and auras and hers is just BLACK!!. Black as the abyss. Everything about her is horrible and vile. She just rubbed me the wrong way every time I was around her, plus she used /still does say the vilest things about me.

She has the same aura as my grandma Nelly, she is a horrible woman but I still love her. Family sticks together right.

"Nah it's definitely not her, but she has been mentioned in my convo"

"Ok so if it's not her then who is it?"

"Troy". She said while huffing and puffing

"Troy? Are you talking about the same guy whose party we went to?"

"Yup the same one"

"Oh ok, sooooooo. What you guys talking about?"

"This and that, but he wants to see me right now"

"Right now?"

"Yes, right now"

"How is that even possible if were in Nottingham and his in Birmingham?"

"He's not in Birmingham, he's Not......" She mumbles

"Nah sis, don't mumble, say what you said with your chest"

"I said his in Nottingham, in fact his right over there"

She said while rolling his eyes and pointing across the road. I looked across the road and low and behold there he was standing next to a black BMW. I never knew what model car it was but the car was beautiful.

Also standing next to the car was his brother, he looked so handsome the way the sun hit his perfectly sculpted body. The way his tattoo's graced his skin, it was like a work of art. He had muscles on top of muscles, it was the most amazing piece of art I have ever seen. His waves were deeper than the ocean, I felt sick just looking at them. His beard was so thick and full, I could see myself holding on to them and going for a dirty ride if you know what I mean. He reminded me of a grizzly bear but a sexy grizzly bear.

"Bitch, so you really plotting on me?"

"Whose plotting? Nobody's plotting on you. I just wanted to see him today and he wanted to see me and since we were both in Nottz it was just easier to link up. Now get out the car and stop being scary."

I was not being scary, I just never wanted to be around him right. The conversation we last shared still resided in my brain.

"I'm not being scary; I don't like being ambushed and you know that"

"No one is ambushing you" she huffed "I know how you feel sis, I know why you're acting this way if it's that hard to be around him right now then u can just stay in the car while I go and talk to Troy for a second."

"I'm not staying in this hot ass car and sweating out my edges, girl I'll be sweating like a turkey on Thanksgiving Day."

"Wait what? We're not even American, how you going to bring up their turkey day?"

"Cause bitch I'm sweating like them muhfuckers scared of being gobbled up"

"Bitch I can't with you, you play too much."

She said while coughing up a storm due to her laughing so much. I decided to step out of the car with my sister, because as I stated before I was not sitting up in that car while she entertained a man.

As I was walking around the car, I could feel like someone was watching me but I could not see who it was, this made my anxiety skyrocket and I could feel a panic attack coming along. I could feel my palms becoming itchy and my heart was thumping out of my chest. Everything around me started to become mute, I could see my sister's mouth moving but I could no longer hear the words come out of her mouth. I could feel myself slipping into darkness. I tried to walk but I lost my footing and almost tripped on the pavement.

I felt some big strong arms holding me up so I never fell flat on my face. As I looked up my words became lodged in my throat. I was beyond embarrassed. There standing in front of me was Damien looking like a Greek God, with his shirt off I could see his bulging muscles contracting, it looked like he could split a rock in half with them muscles. I could see his lips moving, forming words, my brain was trying to comprehend what he was saying/ what was going on, until it hit me again, I started to scratch my arms. This was a level 6 anxiety attack for me and I was finding it hard to come out of it.

"Krystal, it's ok take deep breaths. Come on, copy me. That's right in. And out. In. Out. Don't look anywhere else, keep your focus on me. All eyes on me"

Did this man really just say 'all eyes on me'? yeah ok Tupac.

"Are you ok?

"I'm better now thank you"

"Sis are you ok?"

My sister came rushing towards me with my bottle of water. I felt so embarrassed. I had all these people staring at because my stupid ass had an anxiety attack. Fuck my life.

"Umm Damien, what are you doing? Why you got your hands on this burnt biscuit?" The unnamed woman said so rudely.

"Bitch who the fuck is you calling burnt? You wish your skin was rich like hers. Say another thing about my sister bitch and I'll cut your head off"

This unnamed plastic fake Barbie doll must not have known if she continued to insult me that Katrina was 5 seconds away from turning into, she-hulk and actually ripping her head off and to be honest I would not have stopped her this time. This time I would have joined her because I was ready to beat her ass myself, which is something I would not normally do as I'm more of a reserved kind of woman, but this light bright woman was taking me there.

"Nah sis you don't even need to get involved cause the bitch itching to get slapped" I then turned my head and spoke to Damien. "Who is this woman and why is she being so disrespectful?"

"Bitch don't address my man with your burnt black plantin skin. address me if you want to know who I am" said the plastic barbie doll.

I literally had to hold my sister back with all my might, because if I let her go, we would definitely be making the 6 oclock news tonight. Fighting to keep my sister from killing the barbie doll was proving to be harder than I thought it would be. So much so that Troy ended up coming to my rescue.

" Bro, come sort your pit bull out. She is being way too disrespectful around here!" Troy shouted while giving the barbie a menacing look, almost as if he wanted to kill her there and then.

"Pit bull? nigga are you out your rabbid ass mind?" she replied while sounding as if his words had cut her like a knife. She looked like she wanted to cry there and then.

"Yes bitch you look and act like a fucking pit bull, always trying to go off on people. I don't know what my brother ever saw in you. Your toxic always have been always will be, and I thank God for the day when Damien finally saw through your bullshit when you tried to trap him into having a baby with him. Talking about you taking your injection, you forgot who works in that doctor's surgery? Yeah that's what I thought. He only keeps you around for a good dick suck since that's all your good for and I should know cause that's what I use you for as well"

I'm not even going to lie. I felt sorry for her at that point but then again she kind of deserved to be knocked down off her high horse. I was stuck on the fact that she really tried to trap him into having a baby, like who does that? Ladies trapping a man wont keep him if he's going to leave he will leave no matter what you do no matter how much you beg and plead he WILL LEAVE.

"Are you going to let him talk to me like that?" she said on the verge of tears."And Troy you're a damn lie and I don't know what you're talking about. I've always been on the shot. I don't know what you're talking about!"

"Look I don't have time for this bullshit. Krystal, let's go. And Damien, your a damn fool for letting this dog talk to my sister this way, nigga keep your dog on a leash next time or don't speak to my sister at all. Troy i'll holla at you when i reach back to Brum"

And with that we both travelled to the car and drove away. The car ride to Grandma Nelly's house felt as if it took forever to get there. I kept stealing glances at my sister to gage what was going on through her head at the moment. I could tell she was disappointed in me for not really standing up for myself. I guess we could blame it on Grandma Nelly, every time I stood up for myself when I was younger she always managed to knock me down and make me feel lesser about myself then I did the previous day. Two right turns later and we reached our grandmother's house. I guess Katrina could feel my anxiety starting to raise up because she put her hands in mine.

"Sis it's ok just remember there is nothing she can do to hurt you anymore. remember I got you ok."

I nodded my head and we headed out the car and walked up the steps. Upon reaching the door I could smell the food she was cooking and my mouth started to run water.

"Grams, I can smell that food cooking from all the way outside. What are you cooking up in there old lady?" Katrina asked.

"Now Katrina, I'll beat your ass like I used to beat Kyrstal's burnt ass"

I shake my head thinking to myself I've not even fully made it into the house good and she's already trying to dig at me and bring me down.

"Grams man come on stop that. We all know my sister's not burnt, her skin is beautiful. Plus we both know you're not going to beat me. Since you got that new hip, you slow like a sloth "

Katrina turned her head to look at me and gave me a cheeky wink. Katrina went up the stairs while I carried on into the kitchen where I knew my grandmother would be.

"Hey grandma, how are you doing? the food smells lovely"

"Humpf child I'm fine. And of course the food smells lovely. I'm cooking it, and since you're here I'm guessing you're staying for dinner as well?" with her hands on her hips she rolled her eyes.

"Yes grandma, I came all this way to see you so yes I'm staying for dinner"

"Listen here child don't get cheeky with me do you hear me. I'll beat u like I used to beat you tar baby don't fucking piss me off. You got my baby standing up for you and disrespecting me over your burnt ass. I wish Aaron would have knocked some sense into you, you little disrespectful ass bitch."

"Grandma I'm not trying to disrespect you, I was just saying that I came here to see you, and if you're offering me some food I would appreciate it. Plus grandma can we not talk about Aaron, his locked up for that reason anyway"

Grandma Nelly was about to say something when we heard Katrina scream.

"WHAT THE FUCK!!!!"

Katrina came bolting down the stairs, her face was fire red, spit was flying out of her mouth. she was literally foaming from her mouth.

"Grandma what the fuck is Aaron doing here?!"

As if time had stood still the air around me had become so thin that I thought I could not breathe. Questions kept flowing in and out of my head. Did she really just say Aaron? Aaron can't be here, he is locked away isn't he? Why is he here? Why is he at Grandma Nelly's house?

My palms began to turn sweaty and my heart was beating a thousand miles a second. I turned around and there standing behind me was the devil himself Aaron.

Chapter 5

Katrina

I had to walk away from my grandmother, and mentally check out of the conversation. She can be a real bitch sometimes especially when it comes to Krystal. I my grandmother I really do it's just sometimes well not sometimes 95%of the time she can be a raging bitch and I guess that's where I get my anger from. My grandmother never really came down hard on me and I knew the reason why she always came down hard on Krystal. It was a fucked up reason as well. It took me years to try and wrap my head around it. My grandad was actually Krystal's dad. Let me explain it in more detail, I can see your brains working. My grandad is not my real grandad, he married grandma Nelly when my mom was 15 years old and then divorce my grandma when my mom was 20 years old.

In between those 5years everything was fine, everyone got along from what I've been told. Until one night grandma Nelly came home from church only to find grandad Issac laying on top of my mom. I don't know the details of what happened after that but what I do know is that grandma Nelly continued to let him stay with them even though she knew what her husband had done to her daughter. Grandad Issac continued to attack my mom until one day my mom came home from college complaining that she was feeling sick and her stomach was hurting her. They all ended up at the hospital because by this time she was screaming in pain and was now bleeding. Naturally everyone thought she was just having a really bad period cramp until the doctor uttered those three words nobody was expecting to hear YOU ARE PREGNANT. My mom was 5months pregnant with my sister Krystal, and as you can guess it grandad Issac was the father.

My grandma and grandad would have big blow ups about it, until one day when my mom was 38weeks pregnant and her water broke and blood was coming out of her. She was rushed to the hospital, she was ok and so was my sister Krystal Amari Richardson. I bet you're thinking if my grandad is Krystal's dad is he mine? and the answer is no he is not. When Krystal was 1 and half years old my mom met my dad and he moved my mom out of my grandma's house and I was created. It was beautiful bliss until one night my grandad came over to the house demanding to see his daughter. By this time Krystal was 6 and I was 5years old. A big fight broke out and then we heard a big bang. My memory is a little hazy but I think it's my mind protecting me on those particular details, all I know is grandad Issac is in jail for life and Krystal and I went to live with grandma Nelly.

I bet you're thinking how I knew all the little details before I was born. Well it's because I found my mothers diary she used to keep when she was a little girl, plus one night grandma got flat out drunk and I asked her and she told me everything. She hates Krystal because she represents the betrayal of someone she loved, plus on top of that grandad Issac liked the darker skinned females hence why he went for my mom. I know fucked up right. I can never tell my sister that she's a product of rape, she already feels low about her skin colour. Could you imagine what she would feel if she knew she was a rape baby?

I reached the top step and headed to the bathroom when the door opened up and out walked Aaron. A shocked look crossed my face which quickly turned into a look of disdain. Who the fuck let this nut bag out of jail and what the fuck is he doing in grandma Nelly's house?

"WHAT THE FUCK!"

"Sup sis-in-law you missed me?" Aaron asked with an evil smile on his face. I could feel the evil pouring out of his pores and a cold icy shiver graced my skin.

"What the fuck are you doing here? you're meant to be locked up"

"As you can see I got let out and I'm here because I wanted to see my baby, and by the tone of Ms Nelly's voice I'm guessing she's down stairs"

Both of our eyes made contact when he looked down the stairs, so I made a decision and I bottled down the stairs to protect my sister but I was too late. He had already reached her before I did. I watched him as he kissed my sister's check and placed a hand underneath her chin.

"Hey baby, did you miss me? I sure missed you"

Krystal stood there frozen with fear, I could see the tears well up in her eyes. I had to jump into action and save my sister.

"Mother fucker, don't touch my sister, get away from her!" I screamed and gave him a great big shove which resulted in him tumbling into the dinner table and knocking over the baked macaroni and cheese. For a split second I was sad that I had made him knock over the mac and cheese, but then I remembered why and how it fell on the floor.

"Baby are you ok?" grandma Nelly asked

"Baby?"

Krystal and I both scrunched up our faces with a confused look, did our grandma really call him baby?

"Grandma what the fuck are you doing ? why is this piece of shit in your house and why are you calling him baby?"

"Little girl don't question me in my own house. Do you pay the bills here? No you do not so don't ask me anything"

"Fuck that grandma, why is he here? How could you let him into your house after what he has done to Krystal? Especially after he beat her black and blue and broke her ribs and not only that he beat a baby out of her. This man was high key destroying your granddaughter and you let him back into her life!"

I could not contain my anger. Every single fiber in my body was buzzing like a hornet in a hornets nest. My body felt as if any minute I would turn into the Incredible Hulk and Hulk smash their asses.

"Are you still telling this lie Krystal? You're just like your damn mother"

"LEAVE MY MOTHER OUT OF THIS! How could you Grandma, how could you bring him here? And what lie did I tell!?" Krystal shouted while lifting her top up to show our grandma. "Do these scars look like a lie, do they look self-inflicted to you? I knew you hated me but this is an all time low even for you. You would seriously let this man back into my life just to tortue me even more than you have done?" with tears rolling down her eyes she turned towards Aaron. "And you, you piece of shit, I loved you like I have never loved anyone else and you took everything from me."

"I never took anything you didn't allow me to take," Aaron said with a sly grin on his face and a wink. "plus baby girl you owe me for the last few years I've been away" he tried whispering that part in her ears but I heard that and I saw him grab her arm.

"You should have done more than beat her black and blue, you should have killed the bitch. I know that baby was not yours. She's a hoe just like her lying ass momma used to be. I was glad the day Issac killed her, talking about *my* man raped her. Nobody wanted her burnt black ass anyway, always walking around with no clothes on, flaunting it in his face teasing *my* man. Then she had the audacity to try and tell me that that baby she was carrying was his. Issac told me how she kept on trying to put her dirty pussy on him even when I caught them in that room together I knew it was all her doing" grandma sat on her chair puffing on her cancer sticks, spilling the secret that I have been hiding from Krystal all these years.

I saw the colour drain from Krystal's face as she came to know what myself and grandma Nelly had known. She was a product of rape. Everything she knew to be true was now all a lie. She believed we both shared the same mom and dad, and in a way we did. Since my dad treated her as if she had come out of his own ball sack. She was his and no DNA test was going to tell him anything.

With tears streaming down her face I grabbed my sister and ran out of our grandma's house. I could hear our grandmother and Aaron laughing in the background. Just before I slammed the door I heard my grandma shout 'Leave the bitch, she needed to be knocked down a peg coming in here thinking she somebody. it's ok baby we know the truth'.

Chapter 6

Krystal

The drive back to Birmingham was a long and unnerving drive. I could feel every emotion, hate, anger, sadness, stress, love, hurt. I could feel it all. Grandma Nelly said some outrageous things about my mother. I don't believe them one bit, but the look on Katrina's face when grandma Nelly said them is telling me that maybe there is some truth to it after all.

What really blew my mind was the fact that Aaron was now out of jail and living with grandma Nelly. Aaron the devil himself was out of jail. WTF!! Why the fuck did they let him out? I can feel myself going into a shell. What the fuck am I going to do?

Reaching Katrina's house I had to ask her the burning question.

"Did you know?"

"Krystal I don't think this is the time-"

"No fuck that! Did you know? yes or no its a simple answer"

"Yes, I knew but it's not what you think. I found moms diary one day while we lived at grandma's house, and I asked grandma one night when she was drunk you know that's the only time we can get the truth out of her; and she told me that it was true and that's the reason why she treated you the way she did. Sis I did not know how to tell you. How the fuck to tell the person you love more than anything that you know the reason why our grandma hates them."

I sat there hearing everything she was saying but the hurt around my heart would not let me understand her point of view.

"Bitch you knew the reason she hated me and for years you kept telling me that she never hated me and it was all in my head." shaking my head I thought about it more. "I can't believe i'm a rape baby and my daddy is my grandaddy" with tears running down my face I cried my eye s out not just for me. I cried for my mother. No one deserves to be raped, especially by your step father. I bet looking at me must have been a constant reminder of the horror that had happened to her when she was younger.

"Krystal, how was I meant to tell you this? I was planning on taking this to my grave" wiping her nose, she was blubbering mess. "Krystal I don't want you to shut me out because of this I know how you are when you feel like you have no one in your corner and trust me I am always in your corner"

"I would like for you to get out my car now please"

"Krystal"

"No Katrina I need you to raise up and get out of my car please, I can't breathe right now and my head is all jumbled up. I need to process all of this. Not just about mom and me being a rape baby and my real daddy being grandpa Issac. Did you forget that Aaron is now out? And I know that he is going to come for me. I need to wrap my head around it all. So like I said, could you please go now. I need to be by myself"

I watched as she slowly took off her seatbelt and prepared to get out of the car. She kissed me on my tear stained cheek while whispering in my ear our mothers words 'you are a queen don't let anyone tear you down always remember that'. As soon as those words came out of her mouth, the flood gates I'd been holding back burst open and waves of grief and resentment came over me like a tidal wave in the sea; it kept coming and coming, Until I had reached my destination. I don't even know how I was able to drive and make it home safely. My parents must have been watching over me and was guiding me home.

I sat in my room trying to rack my brain around everything that has happened today. Almost going to jail trying to stop Katrina from killing a barbie doll, Aaron being in the real world, my grandmother finally telling me the real reason why she hates me, finding out that I was rape baby and finding out that my real father is actually my grandfather…. Yeah I'm still trying to wrap my head around that one.

I tried blaming Katrina for it all but I knew that was not right, she had not done anything apart from try and protect me and doing what our mother had always told us to do PROTECT EACH OTHER.

It had been 3weeks since I had seen sunlight, so I stayed inside my house missing work. I had told them that I had some family issues I had to deal with and I told them about Aaron it's not like they never knew about him anyway. I had to inform them plus they know what he looks like due to his crazy ass always causing trouble outside of my workplace, always causing trouble.

Everyone had tried to get in contact with me, people showing up to my house but I would not open the door for them. I had to dead bolt the doors and stick keys in all my doors to stop Katrina from using her keys to get in my house. I needed a mental break from everything, I needed to be alone. It was the only thing I could do from going crazy and doing something crazy that I knew I would regret. I had done something crazy after I healed up from my wounds that Aaron had given me. I actually tried to kill myself. Thinking the reason why no one loved me was because of the colour and shade of my skin. You see on the news, Shade Room, twitter and facebook black people getting killed, black people being harassed or people children ending their lives due to people making them feel that their skin colour impure.

Shaking off the thoughts of doing something to myself I decided to finally pay my sister a visit. As I arrived I saw a car I did not recognise. I never pondered on it for too long . Lord knows I should have but I really needed to see my sister.

Putting my key in the door I was instantly hit with the smell of weed, I knew something heavy must have been on her mind as that is the only time she smokes and she needs to mellow out. Walking into the front room I could hear voices that were not Katrina's, the voice I heard sounded familiar to me. It was Troy's voice. One thing I've come to notice is you don't find one without the other. As soon as I thought about turning around and leaving her to her company, I bumped into something hard. It was Damien.

"Hey, where have you been?"

"I've been around"

"Well not really, you've not been around your sister in a while"

"How would you know that?"

"Your sister and my brother talk, you forgot about that?" with a raised eyebrow and a sly smirk on his face, he looked at me like that was a stupid question to ask.

"I umm... I heard about what happened with your gran and your ex being back"

"And what exactual did you hear?"

"Not a lot really, your sister never really went into details about it, I was in the whip when she phoned my brother so we drove over here to see what was wrong with her. She was in tears most of the time while she was telling us well, really telling Troy about what happened. Was she not meant to say anything?"

With a puzzling look on his face I left him standing there and went to find my sister. Walking into the kitchen I saw an odd sight. My sister was actually cooking food for someone who was not herself or me. She was really in the kitchen with an apron on cooking dinner for a *man?*

"What's up sis?, nice to see you under better circumstances"

Totally ignoring Troy's comment I headed to my sister with a sour look on my face.

"Why are you telling outside people our business?"

"What are you talking about?" she said with a puzzling look on her face.

With my eyes landing on Troy and his brother, they finally came back to my sister. She gave a small sigh that said it all.

"Sis it's not how you think really, so obviously I was distraught when you basically kicked me out your car" I rolled my eyes because I knew she was exaggering with that one. "Troy rang me to see if we got home safely since I never told him we reached. I was crying to much that he told me to stop what I was doing and to basically open the door for him. I never knew Damien was him. I basically told them that grandma Nelly said some fuck up shit to you."

"You mean she told me the real reason why she's hated me all these years and that I'm a rape baby"

"Yeah that, and basically that your psycho ex boyfriend is out of jail and is now living with grandma" she said while twiddling her thumbs.

"LIsten Krystal, don't have a go at your sister, she just really cares for you, we all do. But on a real we need to talk about this psycho of an ex who's out, now we don't know the ins and out becasue your sister would not tell us; but I saw the fear in her eyes when she was talking about this nigga. Now I know you don't want us *all up in your business* as you have stated before, this is some real shit. Now tell us what happened."

The way this nigga just got me together all the way together, made the seat of my biker shorts wet up, and yes a bitch not wearing any underwear cause who the fuck wears them anymore.

Listening to what Damien said I decided to tell them everything that happened at grandma Nelly's house and everything that happened in my relationship with Aaron. We sat there for over 2 hours during that time we ate the food that Katrina had made. I could tell by the looks on both Damien and Troy's face that they wanted to go to war for me, but this was not their fight it was mine.

"I just want to apologize to you now for the comment that I made the night of Troy's party. I can understand now why you have been the way you have been with me" I nodded my head accepting his apology.

"Ya grams is rah vile for the things she put you through, the both you of" Troy said while turning to face Katrina "Is that the reason why you feel that way about yourself?"

"What are you talking about?"

Yeah what was he talking about. Katrina doesn't feel any type of way about herself. I know for a fact, she's the most confident person I know. Right?

"What are you trying to imply?" I really wanted to know, since the look on Katrina's face was telling me that I never knew my sister at all. "Katrina, what is he talking about?"

With a huff she put her glass of white wine down on the counter top. I could tell by the look on her beautiful face that she was finding it difficult to find the words to speak.

"Your.. Your umm not the only person who has issues with their skin tone"

"What do you mean?"

"Grandma used to bully you about your skin, but it also made me hate mine. You wish you were lighter while I wish I was darker like you. To me your skin tone is perfect, it's beautiful, you know this because I tell you this every day."

"I don't understand why you would feel this way?"

"Ok so it's like this, you see how social media and all the history text books always talk about how the darker you are the less attractive you are and all that bullshit right? Well what they don't talk about is why they glorify the reason why they like the lighter skinned black people. They don't wanna talk about how our ancestors were raped by the slave masters and they produced lighter skinned black babies or as they used to call it the 'mix breed or halfbreed' babies. You know the saying 'Light is always white'. Every time I look in the mirror I'm always constantly reminded of somewhere along the line one of my ancestors was raped. It makes my skin crawl"

I was stunned by this revelation, I always believed that it was only me who had a complexion crisis, obviously I was wrong. While suffering in public my sister was suffering in silence behind closed doors. My sister was feeling alone, and I was too self to even recognise that my sister was hurting.

"Sis, I never knew you felt like this, why did you never say anything?" I said rushing to her side to wipe her tears away.

"I just put it behind me, protecting you was more important"

"I'm pretty sure I'm the oldest and I should be protecting you, not the other way around" I chuckled while wiping my tears as well.

"Kat, I've told you loads of times that you're beautiful, no matter what skin tone you are. You think if you were ugly that I would have tried to holla at you?" This man was a fool but I'm grateful for him breaking the tension in the room and making us all laugh.

"Nah but on a level Kat, you beautiful remember that" he kissed Katrina's forehead and turned to me "And you, trust me my brother not *trying* to sniff up behind you for no reason. Fuck what your grandma used to say fuck what that low life Aaron used to say and fuck what Liv has to say, and I know your proberly thinking how I know about that just know that it will get sorted with her. Them other people are just sad and have nothing better to do with their life apart from rip up somebody's life who they know is better than them, They want to bring them down to their poor or a life"

"Krystal" Damien said while wrapping his arm around my shoulder "You know I will never let anything happen to you? You have my number now" wait what?

"Wait what? I don't have your number"

"Yeah you do, I slid my number in your phone while you was explaing everything to us" this nigga.

"Nigga what I know you fucking lying, how you know my passcode?"

"It was unlocked" he said with a shrug "But that's neither here nor there, the point is you have my number now don't be afraid to call me for *anything*."

The way he said anything made my heart flutter. Yes this man just took control of my phone and took it upon himself to add himself to my contact list, but in a way I was grateful that he did that because lord knows I would not have the balls to get it myself.

"Bro how the fuck you just slyly access he rphone and drop ya number in her phone like its nothing?" Daimien asked while laughing his head off

"Easy, same way I just did it" not going to lie he had us rolling with that one.

Chapter 7

*K*atrina

Seeing Krystal the other day meant the world to me. I had been feeling low ever since we left grandma Nelly's house. I felt like my sister would never forgive me for withholding information like that from her. I knew it was wrong of me to do that, but I literally just wanted to protect her. She had already been through enough in her life.I had every intention of taking this secret to my grave, but I guess the lord had other plans.

Getting ready to leave work I could not be any happier as I could finally put my feet up and rest. Plus I could not wait til Mr lover boy aka Troy to come see me. At first glance yes I was attracted to his physical form, and yes I wanted my back cracked since it had been _MONTHS_ since i've had my back cracked. It may have started off like that but the more I got to know him the more I understood his mind and his soul. His soul is so beautiful, the tough boy persona he gave to everyone was just a mask. The real him was this smart caring handsome man, his tough boy persona was only for people he never knew which in a way I could fully understand since i'm the same way. Once I let you in you get the real me, not the standoffish person everyone at work and everywhere else sees.

Normally it would take me ages to warm up to a person but with Troy it was different. I go off energies and if I don't like it the first time I meet you then it's game over, you will forever get the standoffish version of me, but when it came to Troy his energy was so pure that it blinded me. At first it was kind of tainted, well I guess it would be after talking up a storm with Olivia. Liv was a mean spirited person who always blamed everything on everybody else, like the fact that she lost her kids. If you ask her why it happened her answer would be ' the school was lying, my kids were getting bullied and they never did anything about it' or their daddies were lying because I never gave them any pussy the last time they came to see us'. Yeah she's one of those people.

Walking out of work I could hear Liv's voice which caused me to roll my eyes. She was standing next to a nice black car, I never knew the model of the car since I'm not interested in that kind of thing. I had to do a double look at the man in the car, no I was not peeping at him. No it was the fact that I recognised who was in the car. It was Aaron. What the fuck was the peice of shit doing at my place of work and what the fuck was he doing with Liv. I may have disliked the woman but if she found herself dating him then I would have to step in and tell her the truth about this man.

Almost reaching my car I heard my name being mentioned but I carried on walking to my car until I heard a comment that made me turn sound and was ready for war.

"I don't know why you're bothering with calling that bitch for. Look what her family did to us"

"Bitch don't fix your mouth to speak on mine when you have no idea what your talking about"

"I know what I'm talking about. Aaron told me everything"

"Of course you would believe him, he has a dick between his legs. You're like a dog with a bone, you'll chase the stick around just like a dog". I said to her, her mouth was hanging open by the comment I had just made. I turned slightly to the left and proceeded to talk to Aaron. "And you nigga, don't be spreading lies about my sister, don't forget I know everything. I could kill you for what you did to her"

"Bitch don't talk to him like that or me and you can go"

"Listen here you little hoe, don't tempt me with a good time I do this shit for fun. I'll make you ask why your sorry ass pappy released such a basic bitch from his nut, I'll also make u wish your nanny swallowed your pappy instead of making your granddad skeet in her cobweb pussy. Don't fuck with me cause I'll have you rethink what is life. I go hard for mine. Dick nor pussy move me unlike the both of you. I'll release some secrets you both don't want out, come fuck with me if you dare."

And with that I got in my car and left.

Putting the salmon in the oven I focused on my loaded seafood potatoes and making my sauce. I had texted Troy on my way home letting him know that I was 5 mins out, and by the time I reached he was pulling up as well. He was in the front room messing with my stereo when I heard one of my favourite songs come on.

I will love you anyway

Even if you cannot stay

I think you are the one for me

Here is where you ought to be

... I just want to satisfy ya

You're not mine and I can't deny it

Don't you hear me talkin', baby

Love me now or I'll go crazy

... Woah-oh, sweet thing

Oh, you know you're my everything

Woah-oh, sweet thing

Oh, you know you're my everything

Yes, you are

Swaying my hips I sang along with the best song ever made. I don't care what you say, this song hits in so many ways. Fully into the song I never noticed the presence of another person had entered my kitchen, until they wrapped their hands around my waist.

"I hear you in here singing your heart out, all off key and shit. What do you know about these songs, little one?" he said while chuckling and kissing my cheek.

"Fuck you, I can sing and why you always gotta bring up my age? You only one year older than me old man"

"I got your old man" he said while tickling me.

"Ahhhh no stop! I'm cooking the food you're gonna make me spill it"

"Alright man," he said while taking a seat at my breakfast nook while sipping on a glass of henny and coke. "You never answered my question"

"What question?"

"How does your young ass know about this song anyway?"

"Oh, well…… It was my mom's favorite song"

"Ahh shit sorry I never knew I can turn it off if you want?"

"No!! don't do that" I said as my voice cracked a little.

"Baby girl come here"

I turned the stove down and turned around and stood next to him. He stood up and took both of my arms and wrapped them around his neck while he wrapped his around my waist.

"Dance with me"

I giggled and agreed to dance with him, we rocked together through two songs. I cried and laughed at what we were doing in the middle of my kitchen. It brought up so many memories of my mom and dad dancing with each other in the kitchen when I was younger.

I closed my eyes and I could see my mom smiling at me and my dad nodding his head in approval. I miss them so much.

"Why you crying baby?" he said while wiping a tear from my eyes

"Just thinking about my parents, I think they would of liked you"

"Yeah?" I nodded my head giving him the approval he wanted.

I went back to finish cooking the rest of the food. The salmon would be ready in 2 mins so I started to plate our food. I placed the seafood mash potatoes and the broccolini on the plate, then I took the salmon out of the oven and placed our pieces on the plates and poured the creamy sauce that I made from scratch onto the salmon and some on the mash potatoes.

There was no sound apart from knives and forks hitting the plate and the occianal moan coming from both of our mouths.

"Babe, this is banging"

"Well there is more over there if you want some more" I said with a smile on my face.

"You already knowI'm going to get some more" he said while standing up and rubbing his stomach

"Your going to get fat if you keep eating so much food"

"You keep feeding me like this and I'll gladly carry on eating. Just call me Fat Troy"

"Don't you mean Fat Alber?" I said while laughing my head off

"Nah I meant want I said my name is Troy not no Albert.

Hey ,Hey, Hey,

It's Fat Troy

And I'm gonna sing a song for you.

And I'm going to show you a thing or two.

You'll have some fun now, with me and only me.

Learning from each other.

While we eat this food....

Na, na , na

Gonna have a good time.

Hey,Hey,Hey!"

You see what I mean, he is a real life clown.

"So, you wanna tell me what had you so bent out of shape on your way home?"

"Ask your bitch what she done to me"

"My bitch? Who are you talking about?"

"You know who I'm talking about. You hollered at her the same day you hollered at me." I spat vemenously

"What she do now?"

"I was leaving work and I saw her talking to someone so I carried on walking to my car until a comment was made so I decided to light her ass up and light up the man she was with"

"What did the man do to you? you can't go around starting shit with random men. What would you have done if that man would have come and tried to beat the fuck out of you?"

"Then he would have been going back to prison"

"Wait what?"

"The man she had with her was Aaron, and I wish the fuck he would of laid a hand on me. My hands don't discriminate. Pussy or dick can catch these hands. I'll go round for round with him, I have a taser and pepper spray on me 24/7."

I got up from my chair and put my plate in the sink and walked right out the kitchen and sat on the sofa. I pulled out my phone and went straight to kindle to see if any of my favourite authors had put out any books yet. I noticed Nicole Jackson, Cion Lee and Diamond D. Johnson put out books. I downloaded 'We Outside' by Nicole Jackson, 'Wishing on a star' by Cion Lee and 'Beretta's World 2' by Diamond D. Johnson. I also noticed Jazz Moore had still not put out her new book, by her facebook group I could tell this new book was going to be good. I already knew the title of the new book it was called 'CHECKMATE'. I was already in the middle of reading her first book 'No Matter The Weather' and I tell you she had a bitch hooked. Them american niggas don't play about their woman. Woii I have to fan myself just thinking about the main character.

I sat there trying to read the rest of No Matter The Weather, when Troy came into the living room I tried my hardest to ignore him, but he came and sat right next to me and took my phone out of my hand.

"Can we talk for a minute?"

"Lol ok Tevin Campbell"

"Girl, how old are you? you have an old soul don't you?"

"Something like that, but what do you want?"

"I want to apologize for coming at you the way I did. I understand why you went off the way you did"

"Thankyou"

"But do you understand what I was saying though?"

"Yes I do. I understand that if it was any other man it could have ended badly."

"No it could have ended badly anyway, if you guys are telling me that this Aaron geezer is as dangerous as you say then why would you start an argument like that with him? Fully knowing that Liv was there as well and we both know that she doesn't like you. Now imagine if he went for you? Do you think she would help you? Do you think she would help fight him off?"

He was making a lot of sense and making some valid points, but I was too stubborn to admit that I might have done something as foolish as this. Especially because he is a known women beater.

"I need you to understand that yes you may have been able to hold your own with him with the weapons that you had with you, but he is still a man. We are naturally stronger than you and we could do alot of damage"

"I hear you, and now looking back on it I was acting on pure emotion and it could have ended badly. They just got me so mad, all I could see was Krystal laying in that hospital and seeing how badly her face was battered and bruised. I just saw red." A tear dropped from my eye and I tried to turn my head so he could not see me wiping my eyes but of course he spotted me.

"I'm here for you, do you hear me?" I nodded my head.

With a finger underneath my chin he kissed me on the forehead and on my cheek. Then his lips landed on mine, I felt the electricity spark in my lips like an electric shock. The kiss grew so intense that I don't remember making it upstairs to my bedroom.

Due to my speakers being connected all over the house I could still hear the music that was playing down stairs.

Hey, girl, ain't no mystery

At least as far as I can see

I wanna keep you here layin' next to me

Sharin' our love between the sheets

Ooh, baby, baby

I feel your love surrounding me

Whoa-oh-oh-oh-ooh, ooh, baby, baby

Makin' love between the sheets

Our clothes were all scattered all over the stairs and my bedroom floor, he laid me ever so graciously on my bed. He left a trail of kisses across my plump breast , down my stomach and all up and down my legs. He stared at my freshly shaven vagina and kissed around it, driving me crazy. He kissed the inside of my legs

. I could hear him inhaling my scent, his fingers dipping into my fleshy meaty thighs. I suddenly felt a finger enter me, my eyes rolled to the back of my head, and then I felt another finger enter me and rubbed on my clit. I was in sheer bliss. On the verge of cumming he stopped and my eyes popped open. I was getting ready to cuss because it had been quite some time since I had received any type of stimulation in a very loooooong time.

I was just about to start bitching when I felt something wet, warm and fat connect to my pussy. His tongue was stiff as a board and was flickering back and forth against my clit. His fingers found their way inside of my pussy and one found its way into my ass hole.

"Shiiiiiit, eat that pussy"

"Mhh this pussy tastes so good. Look at me"

I propped myself up on my elbows, my eyes connected with his. I felt as if he was sucking and looking into my soul and I loved every piece of it. My whole body felt as if I was having a seizure and I knew my body had betrayed me. 1 minute later .

"Aaahhhh ooooooh, fuck I'ma cum I'ma cum"

"Come on baby, you can do better than that. Fix up" he chuckled while slapping me on my leg

"Leave me alone it's been a while"

"Yeah ok, let me see if you know how to arch that back"

"You mean like this?" I asked and proceeded to arch my back like a seasoned pro and began to bounce my ass cheeks.

In the middle of me bouncing my cheeks I felt his fat tongue again but this time it was not only on my pussy, his tongue was also connecting with my ass hole. I screeched and pushed my backside more into his face than it was before.

He stood and leaned over me to plant a massive wet kiss on my lips. I gladly took his tongue into my mouth and I sucked on his tongue giving him a preview of how I would treat his dick. Moving from my lips I felt him place a little pressure against my pussy. I'm lying it was not a little pressure it was a lot of pressure, I never saw what his penis looked like but it felt long and thick. The best combination to have, all I needed to know if it was veiny then it would be a 3 out of 3 for me.

"Fuck Katrina, you tight as fuck, you wetting my dick up."

"Mmh"

"Fuccck, this mine now you hear me?"

"Mmh yeah I hear you"

"Whose pussy is it?"

"It's yours"

"I can't hear you"

"It's yours"

"What's my name?"

"T Ttttt shitttttt"

Smack!

"What? Is. My. Name?"

"Troy Troy"

"I can't hear you. I asked you a question. What is my name?"

"TROY!!" I screamed and Troy pulled out of me and started to eat me from the back again and a river of water flowed out of me.

"Shit baby" he said while wiping his face. Trying to catch my breath he pulled me on top of him.

"Come ride this dick"

I finally got the chance to see what he was working with and I was thanking god that he was blessed with a long member. It was beautiful and I'm not just saying that because it was covered with my essence, no it was long and thick like a chocolate bar, it also had a slight curve to it, and he knew how to swing that ding dong.

I got on my tip toes and started to rub his magic stick all over my clit.

"Ooh you so biiiiig"

"Come on, ride it, that's it" he said while thrusting me from the bottom and his hands on my hip. "Yeah just like that"

"Fuccck meeee, Troy! Fuck me"

I collapsed on top of his chest and started twerking my fat plump ass on that wonder bone of his. It ended up up in a competition on who could out fuck the other. Position after position we fought for dominance in the bedroom.

3 orgasm's and countless sexual positions later I woke up with a pillow between my legs. My whole body ached but it was a good ache. I brushed my hand across my breasts and a vivid image of our amazing night flashed in my mind.

The buzzing sound on the side table pulled me from my day dream, I went to reach for it and realised that it was Troy's phone that was buzzing. I could hear the shower running so I knew he was in the shower. I was going to ignore the vibrating sound his phone was making but curiosity got the better of me so I decided to take a peak. His phone was locked but I could still see who texted him. I looked at his screen and he had 6 missed calls and 7 messages from Liv. While I was his phone it vibrated again 2more texts came through.

It was from Liv.

'enjoyed r date night the other night'

'Big daddy come round 2morrow i got a surprise 4 u'

Is this nigga really fucking with Liv? Wait are for fucking the same man?

$\mathscr{K}$atrina

Arriving at work my mind was on 10. I parted ways with Troy this morning like nothing had happened. While he was getting dressed I watched him from the corner of my eye, I watched as he looked at his phone and read the messages. He smiled a devilish smile the same smile he gave me last night when I rode his dick while in a chinese split. I watched as he licked his lips and chuckled while responding to her messages. My blood boiled. I felt as if I was a volcano ready to erupt. I had to get out of there. I could not leave my house any quicker especially when he tried to kiss me good bye.So here I am headed to work trying to forget that I want to rip both of their heads off.

Walking on to the shop floor I could sense that today would be a bad day and some shit is going to go down. The first 3 hours of my shift went so quickly and I was loving the fact that nothing had happened. I walked over to my little display that I had set up, I was loving the christmas theme going on, on the shop floor. The gold and red tinsel adorned the walls, the christmas tree had every kind of bauble you could think of on it, it also had fake snow around the perimeter and base of the tree. little reindeers hung from every other branch and the twinkling lights intertwined themselves onto the empty branches.

Hearing one of my favourite christmas songs 'Simply Having A Wonderful Christmas Time' playing through the speakers, I truly felt it was christmas time especially since there was snow on the ground outside and with England we never know when we will get snow around Christmas time.

Every employer had to wear a Christmas jumper or something partaking in Christmas. I opted to wear a little cute elf costume with all the trimmings. I wore the elf dress with the belt, the peppermint striped stockings, the charcoal boots with the fluffy white trim and the hat to match that came with ear's attached to them. It was silly but it put me in the Christmas spirit. As you know it's the most wonderful time of the year.

The day was almost over and I could not wait till I got home. Christmas was only 2 days away, and this year it was going to be different. There would no longer be any tears of sadness or any passive aggressive behaviour, since there would be no grandma Nelly. Grandma Nelly caused all of this on herself. All she had to do was love Krystal the way a grandmother was supposed to, but no, she had to carry all that hate and malicious intent in her cold stone heart.

I know this is going to sound crazy but I miss her in a way. She was a mother to me when mine died, I truly miss the warmth that she gave when I was hurting and missing my mother. I also know that the only reason she gave me so much love is because she hated my sister and everything she stood for.

Walking into the changing rooms I noticed that I was not alone. Standing in the corner at her locker was Olivia. I looked her up and down trying to see if I could find anything repulsive about her, but I could not find one thing wrong with her.

Physically she was flawless, she always came to work looking remarkable. Makeup always on point even if it was a light beat, her hair was always neat, not a whisper out of place. The only thing that was ugly about her was her personality. She reminded me of the grinch but she was like this 24/7. No not the grinch she was more like Hades always has an attitude, just pure toxic energy. So I'm just baffled at what Troy could possibly see in her.

She stood up and walked out the locker room while she did her happy dance, yes I know this girl's happy dance. She only does it for one of two reason's. Either she's going to eat some food or she's about to hop on some dick later. Just thinking that the reason she was doing that dance was because she was going to get some of the glorious pipe I had received last night. It infuriated me.

I decided to let it go and head home. Walking to my car I could see someone posted up against my car, it was a woman I could tell that. Getting closer I recognised the woman, it was Liv. What the fuck is she even doing leaning up agaianst my car. Bitch better get her dirty hands off my car.

"Why are you by car?" I asked her which made her head pop up.

"I'm here talking to you woman to woman, I'm telling you to leave my man alone" is she serious?

"Whose your man? because if your talking about Aaron then you can have that piece of shit"

"Watch what you're saying about him. But no I'm not talking about him. I'm talking about Troy"

"Troy?"

"Yes, you know who I'm talking about. I need you to fall back. Stay away from my family"

"Girl, your family? You reaching now"

"That pregnancy test I sent to him says otherwise"

Pregnancy test? I know this hoe is not pregnant for Troy? I felt my heart skip a few beats.

Before I could even think my feet started moving towards her. I felt like I was having an outer body experience, I was shouting at myself to stop but clearly my body had other plans. I punched that bitch right between her eyes, on impact her left eye immediately swelled up. She staggered back and tried to take a swing at me and I ducked. I was so mad at her that I forgot about her being pregnant, well possibly being pregnant. I was trying to knock that baby out of her rotting pussy. I knew I was wrong to be doing this, but like I said I was having an outer body experience.

In the distance I could hear someone yelling my name telling me to stop, their voice was so chopped and screwed that I could not make out who it was until a pair of strong hands pulled me off Liv.

"Katrina what are you doing? stop"

"Let me go! Let. Me. Go!" I screamed while I was being dragged away. I realised that the person with the strong arms was Troy. He had managed to pull me to his car away from Liv's dusty ass, when I slapped the taste out of his mouth.

"Baby girl no this is not it. I'm not letting you go"

"H hoooow c cccc could you? How could you do this to me?

"Baby what are you talking about?"

"How could you get this bitch pregnant?"

"What are you talking about? Katrina stop hitting me and listen! She's lying it's not mine I've only fucked her once and that was the day I met her"

I know this man was not standing there trying to tell me no bullshit like this. I hate when a man gets caught up in his pimping and some shit they never expected to happen, they come with that dead ass line ' baby the bitch lying' or 'that's not not baby'. It grinds my soul to hear him say this. That's why he was getting these hands.

"Are you serious right now? For her to even claim that she pregnant for you must've been fucking her. How far along is she?"

"Katrina I've not fucked her"

"Don't lie to me!"

"Baby I'm not lying to you" his voice cracked a little. more tears flowed out of my eyes.

"Answer my question!" I yelled while slapping his hand away from my face.

"Bitch you're going to jail!" screamed Liv. I was shocked she was even talking, to be honest I thought she was still unconscious since she checked out of the fight.

"Liv get in your car and go home!"

"Are you serious right now Troy? Are you really going to let this little bitch get away with hitting me and possibly ending our baby's life?"

"Liv shut the fuck up We all know that not my baby!"

"Are fucking kidding me! Was it not you who ran up in me raw 3 days ago?"

Hearing that I punched Troy in his mouth instantly splitting his top and bottom lip. Troy tried to grab me but I managed to slip away from him and I ran towards my car. I could hear both Troy and Liv arguing but I was trying to get out of there as quickly as I could. Driving past them I heard Liv shout.

"This not over bitch watch what happens!"

Chapter 9

Krystal

Seeing my sister the other day really helped me get over a lot of things I had pent up in my chest. It also gave me a lot of clarification on a lot of things. The one thing that I'm still trying to wrap my head around was the fact that Katrina had the same issues as me. Her issues were that she wanted to be darker while mine were I wanted to be lighter. Trying to wrap my head around I could not understand what she was talking about. I loved her shade of brown. It was beautiful. You see all these celebrities bleaching their skin so they are a lighter shade. Not once have I seen a celebrity try and make their skin darker, well that's a lie they can wear a darker foundation but no one has made their skin as dark as mine.

Having told both Damien and Troy everything that happened that day I felt as if some weight had been lifted off my chest. Not a lot but enough for me to be able to breathe a little better.Damien really did help me. After he and his brother left Katrina's house we have been talking a lot. I never thought I would even give him the time of day after that day, but I did something I've never done before. I went with the flow. It was hard at first but little by little I started to relax and feel comfortable with him.

Talking to Damien about everything felt good. I finally felt like I had someone who could actually hear what I was saying. Not saying that my sister never understood what I was saying. Damien overstood everything I was telling him, every mistake I have made, every feeling I felt towards grandma Nelly and Aaron. He even overstood the reason why I stayed with Aaron after the first time he hit me and I stayed. He enlightened my eyes to how I try to look for love and companionship in the wrong places, due to not receiving any from grandma Nelly. Which was true. I thought I loved Aaron because he had a little interest in me. On the other hand I believed him when he used to say 'I hit you because I love you'. When thinking back on him saying that he reminds me of Cross from the film Roxanne Roxanne.

Walking into my front room I turned on my speakers and selected a song from my song, I turned to look into my mirror and started singing at the top of my voice.

"I understand why you wanna try

Make him stay home late at night

But if he wanna go he'll be gone no lie

I can't explain how many times I tried

How many times I cried

Thinking about mine and where he might be (Baby, I don't wanna know)

Remember when I gave everything I got

Couldn't get deep down inside

How you love someone who didn't love me (c'mon)

But now I get if he don't wanna

Love you the right way he ain't gonna

It ain't where he's at it's where he

Where he wanna be

If he ain't gonna love you

The way he should

Then let it go"

I channeled my inner Keyshia cole and I was singing that song like I wrote it myself. I was singing that song *FOR MYSELF.* I just could not shake the feeling I had now that I had seen Aaron. It felt like he had control of me, all the feelings I had for him had resurfaced. I know it was stupid of me to be feeling like this but I could not shake the feeling I had. I felt like he was going to come and see me. So I carried on singing, trying to force myself to let him go and let the feelings I had for him go, because I was really thinking I had Stockholm syndrome.

I grazed my hand over a scar after the last encounter I had with Aaron. I took a deep breath and slid my hands over my face. I was shocked to find out that I was crying. I never noticed it until now. I did not know if it was tears of fear or tears of not being close to someone I once loved. Fuck knows. I guess I'm more messed up than I actually thought I was.

Walking into my kitchen I decided that I wanted something from America to eat, so I went for a shrimp po boy with some fries. I got all my ingredients ready.

1 cup mayonnaise2 tbsp dill pickle relish, 1 tbsp fresh lemon juice, 2 tsp hot sauce, 2 tsp capers, roughly chopped 1, 1/2 tsp paprika, 1 tsp Creole or Dijon mustard, 1 tsp Worcestershire sauce, 2 garlic cloves minced, 3 tsp kosher salt, 2 tsp paprika, 1 tsp garlic powder, 1/2 tsp cayenne pepper, 1/2 tsp black pepper, 2 lbs raw medium shrimp peeled, deveined and tail off, Vegetable oil for frying, 1 1/2 cup all purpose flour, 1 cup cornmeal, 1 cup buttermilk, 3 tbsp hot sauce,4 8 inch long French loaves split horizontally, dill pickles for garnish, shredded iceberg lettuce, jalapenos as I don't like tomatoes and some fries.

The aroma in my kitchen was crazy, my mouth watered like a baby who was teething. I made some red koolaid to go with my food, yes I was going full American cuisine. I could not wait to take a bite out of this.

Before I could take a bite out of my food a message came through on my phone, it was a DM on instagram.

I looked at it and it was none other than Olivia. WTF does this hoe want now.

Today 5:13 PM

 Bitch watch what I do 2 u

Wtf is ur problem?

 U bitch u burnt black bitch fuk u I hope u die

 I hope Daimen dog ur ass out like Aaron did

why are u always coming 4 me? I don't do ur ass anything

 Yu and that hoe of a sister of urs tell her to stay away from my man

What my sister does in her spare time has nothing to do with me

Fuk yuu!!! ur sister a HOE just like U

Seen

 Message...

I don't know what took control over me but I had to let this bitch have it.

Today 5:13 PM

 You guys got something coming 2 u just watch

Bitch fuk u go look after the multiple children by multiple men

Oh wait you cant even do that since u don't have custody of them do yu?

Go eat a dick bitch and get off my phone

Seen

 Message...

With that I ended up blocking and deleting the bitch off my instagram, I don't know why I never had done it before. The bitch was crazy.

Chapter 10

Krystal

Finally finishing my shrimp po boy and kool aid, I went up stairs and decided to run myself a bath. I needed to get rid of all the negative energy Liv just gave me from that DM.

Filling my bathtub with hot water I added some rose bubble bath, baby oil, rose petals and rock salt to help me relax. I lit some candles and poured a glass of wine and placed it on the corner I have for my phone, books and everything else I want while I'm in the bath. I put on some neo soul music to help relax me.

As I was beginning to feel relaxed my phone started to ring, I looked to see who it was. I rolled my eyes and a small sneaky smirk appeared on my face. It was Damien. I dried my hands and answered the phone.

"Hello"

"Hey"

"What's up with up with? what are you doing?"

"I just got in the bath"

"Oh yeah?" I could hear him smiling through the phone

"Nah it's not like that playya"

"Hahaha you're funny, but let me ask you something?"

"What's up?"

"What's got you so stressed out?"

"What makes you think I'm stressed out?"

"Well first of all I can hear the neo soul music playing in the background, plus I bet you got a glass of red wine, roses and rock salt in your bath"

What the fuck? Does this man have a camera in my bathroom? Is he spying on me? What the hell?

"What the fuck? how do you know that?" I asked while trying to cover my breast from any hidden camera's.

"Before your mind goes to crazy town, I don't have a camera in your bathroom. I just remember that from the last time we spoke, you told me that's what you do when your stressed out"

"So what? You think you know me now?"

"Nah I just pay attention and I listen, especially to the people I care about"

"Yeah ok, say anything"

"You're going to learn one day, but any way tell me what happened"

"Some bullshit, Olivia DM'd me on some bullshit talking about how me and my hoe sister need to get fucked up and she said something about my sister needs to stay away from her man. THen she started to go in on the shade of my skin"

"Olivia? Ain't that that bitch who my brother was talking to at one point? And she got that massive backoff?"

"You must have been looking real hard to notice the size of her batty?"

"How can u not see that, that motherfucker is huge"

"Yeah it's huge but it's fake, I'm not even body shaming her but she really looks like an ant" I said chuckling to myself.

"Hahaha baby girl, thats fucked up"

"I'm being honest, you should have seen what she looked like before her 3rd baby daddy gave her some money to get her body done"

Ok guys I can see how this may look, but seriously I'm not hating. This girl was skinny like the Olson twins. She had a pretty face, but that was it. Every time she got pregnant she would fill out a bit but then she would lose it all after giving birth. I think deep down she was never comfortable with the way her body looked and she must have been chasing that high I guess you could say. Once her 3rd baby daddy Tony gave her some money he stole from a bank robbery that he had done, she went and got a BBL and breast enlargement. From the front she looked ok but from the back you could see that her thighs never matched how big her ass was plus her ass **IT NEVER MOVED**!! Deep down I think Tony was the only man she truly loved. I could tell that Tony going to jail for that bank robbery really hurt her, well that and the fact that he had a secret baby with another female, and when he went to trial she came out the woodwork like ' bitch that's my fiance'.

"You low key shady ain't you?"

"Me shady noooo neverrr" we both burst out laughing down the phone "Seriously though if she never got that big of an ass and her breast wa not as huge as they are now she would have looked alright"

"I hear you baby girl. So what do you got planned after you come out of that bath? It has been 2 hours now"

2hours? I clicked on my phone and it really had been 2 hours. We were really on the phone for 2 hours. I got out of the bath and wrapped myself in a towel and sorted out the bath. I walked to my dresser and got my tub of red fox cream and sat on my bed.

"Helloo Krystal"

"Oh shit my bad, I'm still here"

"Ey what are you doing? You finally got out of that bath? I bet your ass looks like prunes now" he asked while chuckling

"Nigga I swear you must have put cameras in my house uno, how you know what I'm doing? Oi I'm going to fuck you up if I find any hidden cameras in my house"

"Haha calm killer, I never put any cameras in your house, I just heard you came out of the bath and sorted it out. Lol you forgot I was on the phone?

"Oh yeah, I guess I did forget that"

We continued to speak while I creamed my skin and put on my blue silk satin eyelash lace trim cami pyjama short set and fluffy slippers. Halfway through our conversation we ended the phone call and ended up talking on Facetime. I felt so comfortable talking to him that I never realised the time.

"Krystal"

"Mhhh" I said sleepily

"Don't you have work in the morning? It's going up to 12 oclock"

"Yeah I do" I replied while yawning

"Go to bed baby girl"

"I am bu…"

Bang Bang Bang

"Yo you ok?"

"Yeah someone just banging on my door"

"Who the fuck banging on your door at this time?!"

"Well if I knew I would have said who it could be"

I got off my bed and wrapped myself with my dressing gown. I travelled down the stairs with Damien still on Facetime. The closer I got to my front door, I felt my anxiety kick in. I had this looming feeling come over me like if I opened this door it would be the last thing I would do.

I opened the door and my mouth dropped to the ground.

"Aaron"

As soon as I said his name everything turned black.

Printed in Great Britain
by Amazon